AS YOU GROW OFF TO SCHOOL YOU GO

Kasey Harris

As You Grow Off To School You Go

iUniverse books may be ordered through booksellers or by contacting:

iUniverse
1663 Liberty Drive
Bloomington, IN 47403
www.iuniverse.com
1-800-Authors (1-800-288-4677)

ISBN: 978-1-5320-7864-4 (sc)
ISBN: 978-1-5320-7865-1 (e)

Library of Congress Control Number: 2019909814

Print information available on the last page.

iUniverse rev. date: 08/19/2019

Great for first timers, school is important. Help your child prepare today with this off to school book!

TABLE OF CONTENTS

INTRODUCTION

I wrote this book for one, because I have always wanted to write a children's book. I am so thankful. I wanted it to be something that all parents and children could relate to. Being able to care for a child as well as watching them learn and grow everyday is so rewarding. Knowing that you have been there to help this tiny person achieve things that you didn't know was going to happen so fast, it's amazing the feelings you develop, and we can not stop our emotions. I wanted my book to be something that touches your heart as you read you see your moments and find your memories in my book while reading with your child. Growing and starting school is a very special time. I hope each child finds comfort through my words. Enjoy

DEDICATION

I chose to dedicate this book to one of my lovely daughters, Jayden Maynard. I made this decision because starting school for you was not so easy. I could see the sadness in your eyes and I felt it just as much as you did every time you did not want to leave me. I wrote this book because eventually you found comfort from teachers, friends, your brother and sisters, and myself that made you feel accomplished and proud. After so long you wasn't afraid and words can not express how happy and proud you have made me. I Love You. I would also like to thank Austin Lovins and Jerry Harris for helping me make this possible. You have no idea how much this means to me. Thank You Mrs. Amy McGehee and Mrs. Sharron Prosser for being there for Jayden. Thank You Iuniverse.

Today is your very own day.
A day full of happiness and love.
The day I've waited for long enough.

You are so tiny, your hands and feet.
You are just beautiful, I am happy
that today we finally meet!

You are perfect in every way.
I will always remember this very day.

I'll treat you with kisses and hugs all day.
I can not wait until we can play.

I love how you crawl and to watch you eat.
I wonder what you will do next,
I can't wait to see!

It's only been months, but I've
enjoyed every moment
Just so you know.

You have touched mommy's heart
in more ways than one
And its only just begun.

You have gone from crawling to walking now.
All day we run around and around.
Wait! Can we sit down?

We even flip, run, and roll.
You only stop to nap, then off you go!

You have your own perfect personality,
it's starting to show.

Look at you go fast!
Time does not last!

Can you believe you are already four!
You have learned so much from colors
and numbers to tieing your shoes.

How did you ever get so big?

You have done so well with all you do.
I think it's time I tell you the BIG news!

You get to go to School!
You can show everyone how much you know.

And you will learn even more as you grow.

Today is your first day.
We walked hand in hand.
I held my tears back as you walked
away, only because of how proud
I am to watch you go today.

You are so sweet and so smart.
You're sure to win friends over
with your big heart.

So, although you and mommy have to sometimes
be apart, I will always be there for you.
As I was right from the start.

ABOUT THE AUTHOR

My name is Kasey Harris. I have always had a passion for writting. My biggest inspiration are my four children. Every day I get to watch them learn and grow so for my first book I wanted to introduce similar moments that we as parents all share and put them into writting.

ABOUT THE BOOK

Starting School for the first time is ALWAYS exciting, emotional, and will definately make you shed a tear. This book is addressed to those who are new to school or preparing for school. I aim to point out the emotions or situations we as parents find ourselves in starting from the very beginning.

Printed in the United States
By Bookmasters